THE RACE

The Grands

written by Suzette Perez-Tate and Anisa Delaluz

illustrated by Hayley Moore

kate butler
BOOKS

First Edition

This book is dedicated to my granddaughter Charlotte Rose Smith and in memory of my mother Norma V. Perez

My mother's bond with my own daughter modeled the precious bond between a grandmother and granddaughter that I looked forward to having with my own one day. Today my relationship with Charlotte means the world to me and I cherish every moment spent with her whether it is long distance or in person. She inspires me every day.

Today is **Gorgeous Grandmother's Day!**

Gorgeous Grandmother's Day is a very special day that is celebrated on July twenty-third.

It is a day we get to show our grandmothers why we appreciate them.

There are many ways to celebrate our Gorgeous Grandmothers.

The Grands celebrate Gorgeous Grandmother's Day
by running in an annual charity race.

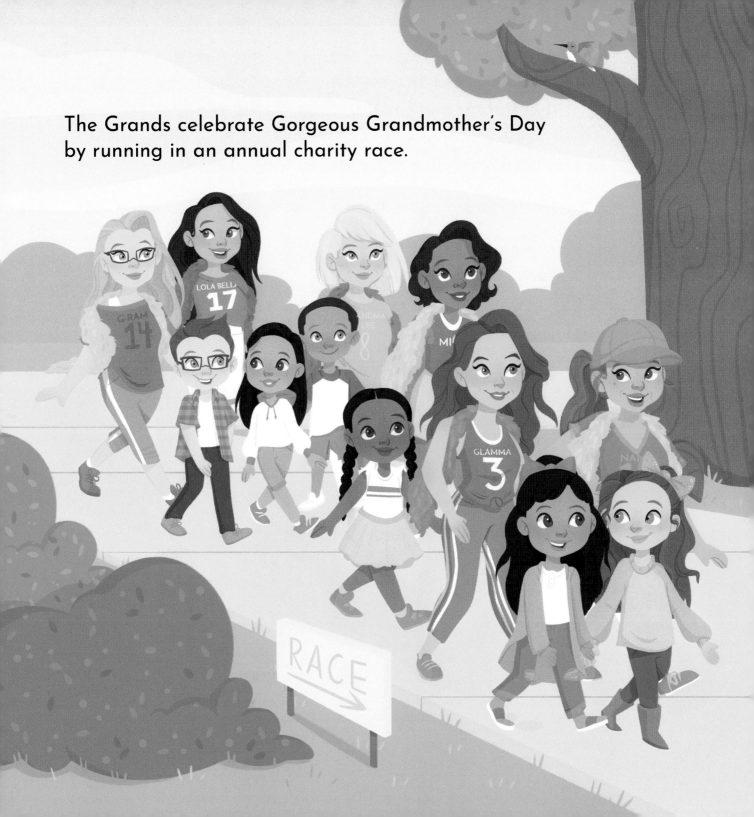

The Grands are six best friends, who became grandmothers at the same time. Gorgeous Grandmother's Day is one of the few days of the year they all get together and spend time with their grandchildren. This is a real treat!

Suzette   Maria   Sheri   Luna   Isabella   Diane

Who do you like to spend time with?

Look, the race is about to start! The grands are fun and playful, just look at their pink jerseys and matching pink boas! Do you see the names on their jerseys? The grandchildren use these special names for their grands!

What special name do you call your grandmother?

The grandchildren are at the finish line.
Can you read the signs they are holding?

With smiles on their faces and joy in their hearts, the grandchildren
are ready to cheer the Grands as they start.

On your marks, get set, **GO!!!**

The whistle blows and off
go the Grands!

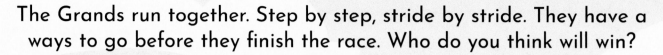

The Grands run together. Step by step, stride by stride. They have a ways to go before they finish the race. Who do you think will win?

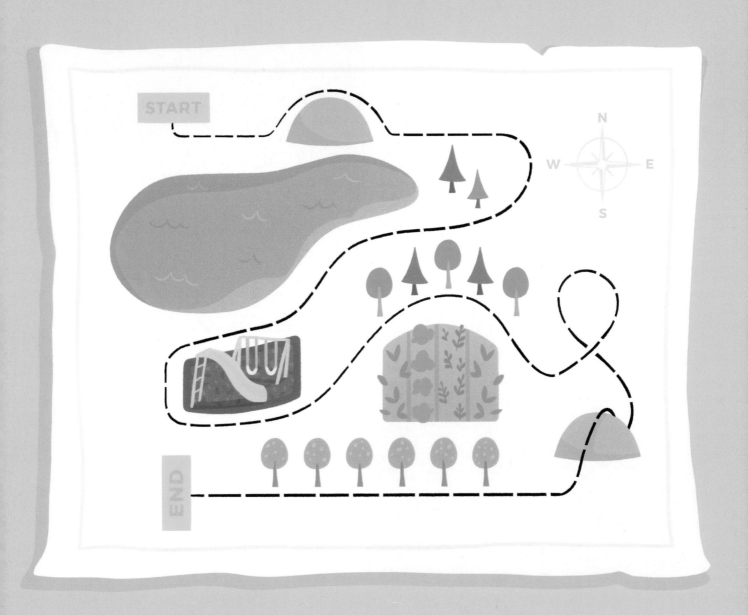

Here is a map of the race. Jordan drew it.

The race is off to a good start. Up the hill they go!
Nana is smiling brightly as she inches into the lead.
Running in the charity race was her idea. The wind carries her laughter.
Charlotte is her granddaughter. Can you see how they look alike?

Hi, my name is Charlotte.
Look at my Nana go! She lives in
California, and I live in Arizona. I don't
get to see Nana as often as some of my
friends see their grandmothers.
We try our best to stay in touch.

The Grands are running past the lake. Right next to Nana is Glamma. Glamma's hair is always just right. It was her idea to add the pink boas. She has style, and so does her granddaughter Sofia, who always wears a bow in her hair.

Hi, my name is Sofia. I call my grandmother Glamma. Doesn't she look great! She might win the race! We spend a lot of time together. Glamma watches me after school until my mom and dad are done with work.

The Grands are passing the playground. Grandma Lee is catching up to Nana and Glamma. Her cheeks are bright pink. She chugs along, excusing herself as she passes the other racers. It was her idea to put their names on the jerseys. Grandma Lee is Jordan's grandmother. They both have dimples when they smile.

Hi, my name is Jordan. I call my grandmother Grandma Lee. Wow, she looks like she's having fun! Grandma Lee moved closer to us after Grandpa Lee died. She comes to our house often, and we do many activities together.

There's a new leader in the race as the Grands pass the little garden. It's Lola Bella! She's looking fit! She led the Grands with their warm-ups before the race. Izzy is Lola Bella's granddaughter. They share the same name.

Hi, my name is Isabella, but I like to be called Izzy. I'm named after my grandmother, who I call Lola Bella. Lola Bella practiced a lot for this race. I live in her house with my Mama and Daddy when he's home from the Navy.

MY LOLA BELLA IS AWESOME!

Around the bend, and down the hill, Lola Bella is still ahead. Close behind her is Mimi, who is quite precise with her steps and her breaths. Mimi made sure all the Grands drank enough water before the race. Alex is her granddaughter. They're both always asking, "How?" and "Why?"

Hi, my name is Alex. I call my grandmother Mimi. She's breathing through her nose and mouth so enough oxygen can flow throughout her body and help her run longer. You see, Mimi and I do science experiments together. She believes it's important that I understand how things work.

Moving out of last place and surprising everyone is G-Ram. She's huffing and puffing, but she is not giving up. G-Ram made healthy snacks for everyone before the race. Jake is her grandson. They both have blue eyes.

You can do it, G-ram!

Hi, my name is Jake.
I call my grandmother, G-Ram!
I didn't know she could run so fast!

G-Ram is taking care of me while
Mommy is away for a little while.
G-Ram makes sure I get to talk
to mommy every day and takes
me to visit her once a month.

Still huffing and puffing, G-Ram is now out in front. She is past the row of trees. **Wait one second!** Nana is catching up, smiling, and laughing. Behind them is Mimi pacing her steps.

Glamma is close by waving her pink boa. Grandma Lee is not worried. She's keeping up. Lola Bella makes the race look like a breeze.

At the finish line, the grandchildren cheer. Go Nana! Go G-Ram! Faster Lola Bella! Yay Glamma! Keep it up, Mimi! Woohoo, Grandma Lee!

But wait! The Grands are running all together - side by side, and stride by stride. They can see their grandchildren's faces and their signs.

One more step, and they all tie! They do this every year. It's not about winning. It's about celebrating being Grandmothers. They hug their grandchildren, Charlotte, Sofia, Jordan, Izzy, Alex, and Jake.

Did you think that was how the race was going to end?

The race is now over. This has been the best Gorgeous Grandmother's Day yet! The Grands and their grandchildren celebrate at their favorite restaurant.